A Little Fawn Grows Up

by Kris Bonnell

Spring is here.
The little fawn is
a baby.

The little fawn hides in the grass so he will be safe.

Summer is here.
The little fawn likes
to run and play.

He eats a lot of grass so he will grow big.

Fall is here.
The little fawn hides
in the trees.

The road is not safe
for the little fawn.
He will go back
in the trees.

13

Winter is here.

Look at the snow.

Where did the little fawn go?

Here he is!

He is all grown up!